Written by Helen Greathead
Illustrated by Amerigo Pinelli
Designed by Sarah Allen

First published by HOMETOWN WORLD in 2011
Hometown World Ltd
7 Northumberland Buildings
Bath BA1 2JB
www.hometownworld.co.uk

ISBN 978-1-84993-190-8

Spooky
DEVON

Written by Helen Greathead
Illustrated by Amerigo Pinelli

HOMETOWN WORLD

Creepy Contents

Welcome to Spooky Devon...

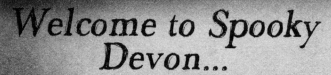

So you think you know everything there is to know about Devon? Have you ever wondered what mysteries lie hidden from the bustling crowds? The stories you are about to read are all set in real places around Devon at different times in the county's colourful past, and inspired by real reports of ghostly sightings.

Devon today is a popular and busy holiday destination. But for hundreds of years many of the fishing villages, market towns and moors remained much the same. Some of these places are steeped in history and some are said to be haunted by their past. Maybe you have felt an eerie presence at Exeter Cathedral...or paused beside an old cottage with the funny feeling that you are being watched. Perhaps you've travelled by car across Dartmoor and felt a hairy hand on your shoulder or visited an old inn packed with eerie old objects from the past. Read on, if you dare, to discover the ghastly goings-on and spooky spectres that may haunt your neighbourhood.

Whooo's Who

Vanishing Nun

Died: January 26, 1833
Favourite Haunt: Exeter Cathedral
Sound: Silent
Sightings: Usually at 7pm during July
Special feature: Walks through walls.
Chill Factor:

Hairy Hands

Date: 1925
Sound: Silent
Favourite Haunt: B3212 road, Dartmoor
Sightings: Unconfirmed
Special feature: a pair of hairy hands...and no body!
Chill Factor:

Unknown Sailor

Age: 170 years ago
Favourite Haunt: The Highwayman Inn
Sound: Calls 'Diana'
Sightings: Unconfirmed
Special feature: Black, frost-bitten fingers.
Chill Factor:

Spanish Girl

Age: 400 years old
Favourite Haunt: Torre Abbey, Torquay
Sound: Sobbing
Sightings: Many
Special feature: Dressed in boys' clothing.

Chill Factor:

Slave Boy

Age: over 200 years old
Favourite Haunt: 46 Cowick Street, Exeter
Sound: Silent
Sightings: Several
Special feature: Appears as head and shoulders.

Chill Factor:

Ragged Boy

Died: 150 years ago
Favourite Haunt: St Vincent's Cottage, Lynton
Sound: Silent
Sightings: Unconfirmed
Special feature: Chased by an old hag dressed in green.

Chill Factor:

Old Hag

Age: unknown
Favourite Haunt: St Vincent's Cottage, Lynton
Sound: Silent
Sightings: Several
Special feature: Dressed in green

Chill Factor:

Spooky Devon

Read on if you dare...

The Minstrel's Gallery

According to local legend, on a warm summer's day in July, you may spot the ghost of a nun appearing and disappearing through walls in and around Exeter Cathedral...

Charles Nosworthy was probably the most irritating boy Harry Endacott ever had been unlucky enough to meet.

And the dislike was mutual, because Charles, who looked like a giant next to Harry, thought Harry was a little squirt who should never have been allowed over the threshold of the cathedral.

The cathedral in question was Exeter, where the boys were rehearsing the All-Schools Concert for a large audience of people from all over the city that same evening. Children from schools around the city had come together to form the choir, and St James's Community College was proud to have Harry representing them – he was still only in Year Seven! Loads of the children came from Exeter Cathedral School, and Bramdean, two of the smarter schools in the city.

The Minstrel's Gallery

Harry had made his own way from Whipton to the cathedral. He didn't come to the centre of town often and he'd panicked when he got there. *How could anyone lose a cathedral when there are signs for it everywhere?* he asked himself. But that's exactly what had happened. Eventually he'd slipped along the narrow passage of Martins Lane, and emerged into the vast open square of Cathedral Close.

If it wasn't for the colourful modern chairs and tables outside all the cafes – and the people sitting in them – you might really believe you'd arrived in 14th century Exeter.

The cathedral itself sat majestically behind the green. Harry's dad had told him it was gothic – whatever that meant. There was a huge stained-glass window on the front of the building at the top and stone screens below it were decorated with figures from a previous age. Angels, apostles, kings…

Somehow the building seemed even more enormous on the inside. Harry had stared up at the fabulous ceiling, and imagined the sound of the choir echoing around its painted bosses and curving vaults. He'd thought he might burst with excitement. But that was before he met Charles.

"What are you wearing?" Charles asked scathingly. Harry's school uniform had definitely seen better days. His jumper and trousers were patched at the elbows and knees and the collar of his white shirt was a dusty brown from the play fighting at morning break. Harry felt a tempting urge to punch the great lump of a boy,

but instead he ignored Charles and walked to the other end of the vestry to change.

This was a dress rehearsal, and the first time the whole choir had sung together. Charles was already dressed, but Harry had never even tried on his fancy chorister's robes before. He slipped the bright red cassock over his head. It was a bit on the long side and the white surplice billowed unflatteringly over the top of the cassock. Then, just as Harry had finally managed to press together the Velcro fastening on his stiff, starched ruff, he felt two fat fingers snap it off again. He caught the collar just before it hit the floor and wheeled round to find Charles standing right next to him, his plump rosy cheeks far too close for comfort; his face fixed in a malevolent grin.

"Aren't you a bit small for this lark?" Charles sneered, gazing at the hem of Harry's cassock as it trailed on the floor. "You need a good strong pair of lungs to belt out those hymns and you're nothing but a pipsqueak."

Harry hated anyone making fun of his height, but he chose to ignore Charles again and followed the rest of the singers through a finely carved wooden screen, to take his place in the choir stalls.

The organ struck up a well-known fugue and Harry could feel the music vibrating in the pit of his stomach. He closed his eyes for a moment to soak up the atmosphere. But then Charles was next to him, nudging him and carrying on with his childish taunts. "Bet you're a bit of a scaredy-cat aren't you?"

"No," Harry snapped. This boy was totally unbelievable.

"Bet you daren't climb up on the screen in the minstrel's gallery and dangle your legs over the side!"

"Don't be ridiculous," Harry sighed in reply.

"I dare you. Come on, let's do it now… Or are you chicken?"

"No, I am not chicken," Harry huffed. "But we're supposed to be rehearsing, remember?"

"Right, then, after rehearsal," said Charles. "I'm holding you to it. No backing down now."

"I haven't said yes," said Harry. "And why would I want to do anything with you anyway?"

Charles's face clouded over and he leaned so close to Harry that their noses nearly pressed together. He spoke in a threatening whisper.

"Because if you don't I'll…" Charles glowered.

Harry bent backwards to get away from the bully and, just behind Charles, the dark figure of a furious-looking nun caught his eye. She was glaring daggers at Charles. Harry, still bending backwards, raised an arm to point around the older boy's large frame.

"If you don't behave yourself, I reckon she's going to wallop you one," he said. Charles turned to look, and immediately, the colour drained from him. The woman gave Charles a pinch-faced look that seemed to say, *I'm watching you!* Then she drifted off behind a pillar.

"Crikey! What's she doing here?" Charles quickly straightened up and started paying unnecessary

attention to his song sheet. Harry was relieved. At least the weird old woman had shut Charles up.

The two boys stood side by side in the middle row of the fancy wooden choir stalls. They were quiet for a while. But, as the master raised his arms to get everyone's attention, Charles nudged Harry sharply, making him knock into the girl next to him. The choirmaster threw him a furious glare, and Harry fumed with the injustice of it. It was Charles who should have been in trouble, not him.

At last, the choirmaster flicked up his baton, smiled round at the eager faces of the choristers, and signalled for the first song to begin. Then, something incredible happened. Charles became a different boy. He stared intently at the choirmaster, following every movement of his hand. He pulled surprisingly sweet faces as he sang, and his voice soared with the music, hitting the high notes with delicate ease and sinking effortlessly down again. His voice had an incredible range and the sound he made was almost angelic. Harry was amazed and he even started to wonder whether he'd misjudged Charles. However, as soon as the music stopped, the bully boy was back to his old self again.

"Call that singing? Our old cat was more tuneful than you when I kicked it round the garden."

The same thing happened again and again. Charles sang sweetly with the music, but turned nasty between pieces. By the end of the rehearsal, Harry was starting to wonder whether he wanted to perform that evening after all. It seemed more trouble than it was worth. As he moved towards the vestry, Charles turned to him and glowered.

"Right," he snarled. "Time for our little trip up to the minstrel's gallery, chicken."

On the one hand Harry wanted to prove himself to Charles, but on the other, he didn't want to get into trouble, and in any case, he'd have to rush if he was going to get home for tea and back again by seven o'clock. But the look on Charles's face was menacing, threatening…and at the same time kind of hypnotic. Charles started walking, and Harry found himself following…

There was a small wooden door to the left of the cathedral's famous, 500-year-old clock and Charles pushed Harry through it. *What am I doing?* Harry said to himself, as his heart began thundering in his chest. He tried to turn back, but Charles's hand pushed him firmly forward. Harry was growing more anxious by the second. His brain was working overtime. *Why does Charles want me up in the gallery? What's he going to do there?* Harry wasn't exactly scared of heights, but he wasn't all that keen on them, either. As he climbed each step, his heart thumped harder. There was something about this that just wasn't right. His mind was whirling with possible explanations. And all the time Charles kept pushing him forward, never saying a word.

They'd turned a corner and – "Aargh!" – there, right in front of him, waiting to pounce, was the furious old nun. She wasn't looking at Harry, but her

21

expression still filled him with dread. She was only staring at Charles, and he was shrinking away from her, cowering, as if he expected her to hit him. Instead, the woman pushed past Harry, grabbed Charles by the ruff round his neck and marched him back down the stairs.

Harry let out an enormous sigh of relief and gratitude. With it, he felt his whole body relax. He hadn't realised how rigid he'd been as he'd climbed the stairs. Had he got rid of that horrible boy at last?

Harry kept his distance, but crept down the stairs after him to make sure.

They were a weird-looking pair, the thin wizened nun, her black dress swishing around her ankles, leading the oversized choirboy in his flowing red and white robes, as though she had him on a string. He watched them march across the nave and wondered what was going to happen to Charles. That's when he saw it. He really did, he wasn't making it up. The nun stepped straight into the wall of the south aisle, and disappeared right into it! And then, no word of a lie, Charles, as though still on a lead, was pulled through after her. He disappeared right in front of Harry's eyes – into the south aisle wall.

*No, it can't be true. There must be a door…*Harry said to himself, and he rushed towards the wall, to check. He pushed his hands hard against it. The wall was definitely solid. Even the nearest window was several metres off the ground, and in any case, it was stained-glass and not exactly designed to open.

Harry had been standing in front of the wall with his mouth open for some time when he noticed the plaque. It was marble and looked freshly polished. Its gold lettering glinted in the early evening light.

IN MEMORY OF
CHIEF CHORISTER
CHARLES NOSWORTHY
(1850-1864)
WHO WAS TAKEN TOO SOON FROM THIS LIFE.
HIS SPIRIT LIVES ON.

Harry was having difficulty taking all this in. So the nun and Charles must both have been...ghosts! Harry had never believed in the supernatural...and Charles had seemed so real! Harry remembered feeling the boy pushing him up the steps.

A firm hand landed suddenly on his shoulder and Harry almost hit the high-vaulted ceiling. He turned to see the choirmaster.

"Sad story that one," he said, pointing at the plaque. "By all accounts, young Charles Nosworthy was a very talented boy. He fell to his death, you know, from the edge of the minstrel's gallery. I like to think he's still watching over us..."

Hairy Hands

Out in the wilds of Dartmoor, ancient granite tors provide bleak landmarks from which many legends have sprung. And on one straight stretch of road near Postbridge, several unexplained accidents have happened. Some blame those accidents on a mysterious pair of hairy hands...

Sometimes Carl felt more like the parent than the child. He thought they were just going for a walk on Dartmoor. His dad, Dick Gurney, had other plans.

The stone was light grey and crusty with white and yellow lichen. It glistened with tiny quartz crystals.

"I'll get it in if it kills me." Dick Gurney huffed and puffed as he manoeuvred the stone into the back of his jeep. He was a slight, skinny man, and not particularly fit. His face had turned red as a beetroot with the effort and sweat dripped from his eyebrows to sting his already bloodshot eyes.

One of the stacks of the Tor had collapsed in the night. Dick had heard it on the news, and rushed to take advantage once his day's work was over. He'd dragged Carl along with him, but Carl didn't want to be seen helping.

Hairy Hands

"I've got a bad feeling about this, Dad," the boy said, looking around nervously. "Stones from the Tor are a bit special, aren't they?"

"Nonsense," Dick scoffed. "A stone is a stone, and this one will fit the Penrose's garden, proper job."

Dick Gurney was a builder, who liked to pretend he was a landscape gardener too. He didn't see the point in spending money on materials so he begged, borrowed, blagged and, yes, sometimes even stole them, if he had to.

He'd driven his four-wheel-drive jeep across the moor right up to the rocks of Hound Tor. Then he'd backed up to the fresh clitter from the rockslide and made space for it in the back of his jeep.

The Tor was one of many on Dartmoor. A huge rocky outcrop perched on a hill, it towered over acres of bleak, stunning moorland. Carl wasn't surprised the rocks had slipped. Looking at them now they seemed so perilous. The dark shadow of a cloud scudded over them. He had the distinct feeling they were being watched, though he knew there was no one else there. Carl had read a piece in the *Western Morning News* about Dartmoor Stone. Some local ghost-hunters had a theory that spirits could somehow be preserved in

the granite – a bit like how a photograph captures a moment in time. He shuddered at the thought.

"Let's go!" Dick called. Carl turned, looking at the deep, muddy tyre tracks mingled with sheep's dung, ferns and gorse that now led up to the Tor. He put all thoughts of haunted stones to the back of his mind and climbed back in the cab.

The jeep wasn't much fitter than its owner. It wheezed its way back down to the road, struggling over the hump at the edge of the moor and hitting the tarmac with a crunch.

Carl turned back to check on the rock. It was safely wedged in the back with bags of sand and cement.

He felt a wave of relief as the Tor grew smaller. Carl twisted the metal knob sticking out of the radio, where the button used to be, and was greeted with a crackling, buzzing noise.

"Turn that blasted thing off," his dad complained. "I can't concentrate on driving."

The air outside turned colder and spots of rain began peppering the windscreen. Dick flicked a switch but only a solitary wiper crawled across the rear windscreen, noisily scraping the glass as it went. The rain grew heavier and heavier. Dick was forced out of the truck to try and fix the front wipers, but they refused to budge.

He wound down the window and drove with his head sticking out so he could see the road.

"Curse that blasted rock," he shouted into the bleak hillside, as rivulets of rain wriggled down his craggy face. "If it wasn't going to save me a small fortune, I'd ditch it here and now."

Carl shivered. He told himself the drop in temperature was down to the rain and the fact that it was getting late.

"Can I turn on the heater, Dad?" he asked, as an icy blast of air whipped round his bare neck, sending a shiver zigzagging down his spine.

"You can if you must, but it'll do no good while the window's open." The heater didn't make any difference. Just like the radio, it fizzed a bit, then didn't work at all. Carl pulled the old, smelly dog blanket round his shoulders, while Dick said a few words that shouldn't be written in this book.

"Mum would tell you off for saying that, Dad." Carl said quietly.

"A saint would blasted-well swear if he had to put up with this!" Dick shouted into the wind.

"A saint wouldn't have taken the rock from the Tor in the first place." Carl's dad didn't hear him above the noise of the rain and the splutter that had just developed in the engine.

"Now what's wrong?" Dick cursed even harder, but the truck was still moving, so he didn't stop to look.

Darkness was falling as the road wound its way through the ancient village of Widecombe-in-the-Moor. The old stone buildings looked deserted without coachloads of tourists wandering around.

Dick drove along a one-track lane with tall hedges and tight passing places, then turned onto a road that led across the open moor. The jeep bounced up hill and down dale, splashing through deep, wide puddles as it wound its way back to – actually, Dick hadn't

looked at the road signs. He wasn't
all that sure where he was going.
He turned on the
headlights, but the

beams of light
were so dim they hardly
made a difference. They chugged on
down the road, the rain pounding, the engine
coughing, Dick cursing and suddenly – nobody flicked
a switch – the headlights gave out dazzling, full-beam
light. There was a B-road ahead, and the headlights lit
up a sign pointing to Postbridge.

Dick cheered up now that the headlights were
working properly. The rain began to ease, the wipers
even sloshed across the windscreen a couple of times.
There was a sudden blast of burning hot air from the
heater. Even the engine quietened. It was good to
be on a proper road again, a nice straight one, with
simple grass verges, ditches, lifeless trees and low

stone walls on either side.

As they sailed through Postbridge, Dick sat back and gave a sigh of relief. "It'll be plain-sailing from here all the way to Princetown."

Carl wasn't so sure.

"I hope so, Dad," he whispered. He had the strangest sensation that his dad really wasn't in control. Something was making these things not work and then work again...but what?

Carl tried telling himself not to be stupid, but then the radio started up again. It crackled and squeaked at first, but there was definitely a voice in the background.

"Tune it in, Carl," said Dick. "See if you can get Radio Devon, or Plymouth."

But the radio didn't need tuning in, because suddenly a voice came over the airwaves, loud and clear.

"Dick Gurney, Dick Gurney, Dick Gurney," it boomed, over and over. This wasn't a DJ playing a request for Dick's birthday. The voice sounded evil, angry...and vengeful. It was as though something was in the jeep with them.

Dick hadn't noticed the hands slipping down his shoulders and along his arms. He hadn't felt their icy touch, though the heat in the cab was roasting. He didn't see the hands take hold of the wheel and, in any case, what could he have done?

Carl was nervously looking around for a body to put the voice to when the truck suddenly lurched to the left. He spun round and that's when he saw them.

Next to his dad's hands, callused and worn, with scabs and open scratches from the stone, was another pair of hands. Carl's eyes widened in fright. The hands weren't attached to a body! They were huge and powerful, with claw-like fingernails, and covered in hair as thick as fur. The hair was matted with mud, or maybe it was blood? Carl tried to cry out, but found he couldn't make a sound. He gripped his seat as the furry hands yanked the steering wheel and the truck swerved.

Even Dick knew something was up now. Though he couldn't see the hands, Dick knew there was something in the cab, grappling with him and trying to seize the steering wheel.

But Carl's dad was stubborn. He wasn't a man who liked to back down.

The hands pulled the truck in a zigzag pattern along the straight, dark road.

"I'll master this," Dick said under his breath.

"Dad, please," Carl finally managed to squeak. "Get rid of the stone." But, as usual, his dad wasn't listening.

"*I'm* not losing that blasted rock! And that," yelled Dick, "is final!"

The vehicle travelled smoothly for a while, and Dick smiled to himself, convinced he'd won. He would get home safely tonight and take the truck in for a service in the morning. He'd have a great story to tell in the pub. Dick smiled to himself and slid back in his seat, but this was no time to relax.

Hairy Hands

Carl could still see the hands on the wheel.

"Dad," he whispered nervously, "you know the old story – the hairy hands? It's this bit of road, isn't it? This is the part they say is haunted."

"Oh, for goodness sake, Carl," Dick was yelling again. "Give it a rest with your stupid stories." He put his foot down, though, as if he was racing towards Two Bridges, to get onto a different stretch of road.

And that's when the hairy hands took charge. They'd only been playing with Dick before. This time there was no way out for the truck. The hands grabbed the wheel with all the power their invisible shoulders could muster. The truck hit the grass, spun round once, twice, careered into the ditch and flipped over so the tailgate slammed into the low stone wall.

Carl's head started spinning as soon as the truck hit the grass. The passenger door flew open, and he followed it out, landing on his back in the long, damp grass, his feet plonking straight into the watery ditch.

With his head flat against the grass verge, Carl clearly saw the weighty hunk of granite tossed up into the air as if it were a child's pebble being thrown into the sea. The stone seemed to fly through the air with the lightness of a bird, before landing in a nearby field and embedding itself in the bank. No one would ever know it had just landed. It looked as though it had been there for thousands of years.

Carl looked himself up and down, brushing mud from his clothes. There were a few rips in his jeans, and scratches on his jacket, but otherwise he was OK. He scrabbled to his feet. Where was his Dad?

Carl hurried round to the driver's door on the upside-down truck, just to see his Dad beginning to crawl out. Phew! They were both fine. No broken bones.

"I think the jeep's a write-off," said Dick, panting as he collapsed onto the grass.

"I think so too," said Carl. He cast one last look at the stone. It was back on the moor where it belonged.

The Haunted Door

People come from far and wide to see the amazing *Highwayman Inn* on Dartmoor and find out about its ghostly past. The building dates back to the 13th century. Now the inn is crammed with old coach parts, bits of ships and even stuffed animals. Imagine what kind of ghosts you might find there...

D i woke suddenly and sat bolt upright in bed. She felt rigid with cold. It wasn't the normal sort of cold you feel in a draughty old room; it was a bitter, biting, bone-chilling cold. She'd never felt anything like it before. She was shivering uncontrollably. It was the temperature, of course, but it was fear as well. Something very strange had happened in the night, it was hazy, though, she couldn't quite remember...wait...that was it!

Something – or someone – had taken hold of her ankles and tried to drag her out of bed. Had it been a dream? It might have been, but when she thought back, she could really feel the rough, weathered hands, as if they'd left a great burning rash around each of her ankles. She pulled up the legs of her pyjama bottoms to look, but there was nothing to see.

The Haunted Door

When she told everyone the next morning, they all agreed it must have been a dream. But if that was all it was, why did it haunt Di for the rest of the day, and why were her ankles still burning?

Di's parents, together with Di and her little sister, Em, had agreed to look after a pub called the Highwayman Inn, in the village of Sourton, on the edge of Dartmoor. The owners had been called away suddenly, and the family moved in at very short notice.

As they'd pulled up outside the inn, Em and Di's faces lit up with delight. This was no ordinary pub. For a start, you had to step through the cab of an old-fashioned horse-drawn carriage to get in!

Then once you were inside, the inn was dark and dingy, with wood-panelled walls glinting with polished horse brasses and old copper kettles. There were swords on the walls and even a ship's helm on one ceiling! Faces, carved from wood and brass, laughed and leered at you from nooks and crannies. Each door that opened revealed a fresh surprise.

"It's a children's paradise!" Em had exclaimed with excitement, and everyone had laughed because she sounded so grown up.

Di and Em slept in one of the guest bedrooms. The bad news was they had to share a bed. The good news was that it was a four-poster, with curtains you could close to keep out prying grown-ups. The girls had giggled themselves to sleep that first night, happily planning the games they would play the next day. But in the darkness, everything had changed for Di.

On the second night, she was nervous about going to bed.

"I'll swap sides with you," Em offered, "I'm not scared of anything!" It was true. Em might have been the littler sister, but she was the one with guts.

It must have been about three o'clock in the morning when Di woke up screaming. It was dark, she was still wearing her pyjamas, but she wasn't in bed and she was soaked to the skin! And she could feel burning around her wrists this time.

Where was she? Outside? It seemed to be bucketing down with ice-cold rain, each drop as sharp as a needle. She couldn't move, but she kept screaming and screaming. Eventually, a light flicked on and she realised she was sitting in the bath with the shower on full power. Mum was on the other side of the shower curtain, her face confused and concerned, holding a towel.

"You must have been sleepwalking, love," Mum said as she dried Di with a towel and put her back to bed.

But Di didn't think so. She was cold and

frightened and she didn't sleep at all after that. She remembered something else from the middle of the night. A voice. It sounded distant, desperate and it was calling to her.

"Diana, Diana!" it

cried. "Why did you leave me?"

How did the voice know Di's name? And what did it mean about her leaving? She hadn't gone anywhere. When Di told everyone what had happened they assured her she must have been sleepwalking. They said she'd accidentally set the shower off when she'd walked past, knocking the lever. And the voice, well, that was just in her dream...

But if they'd checked, they would have known that Di couldn't have turned on the shower by accident because the lever was too high up. And anyway, Di knew the voice was much more than just her dream. It seemed filled with pain and anguish, and it was far off, as though there wasn't anything she could do to help it. Di felt alone and very frightened. More than anything, she wanted to go home.

On the third night, they went to bed with a howling wind and the beginnings of a storm outside. "There's no way I'll ever get to sleep tonight," Di thought to herself. But she must have nodded off at some point

The Haunted Door

and this time what happened was so much more than a dream…

Di woke to find herself lying on a wooden panel. Her cheek was pressed against its ornately carved surface. She felt the biting cold again. She felt freezing rain stabbing at her skin. The board beneath her was rocking violently, as if buffeted by a gale force wind. And in the distance, the voice was echoing "Diana, Diana! Why did you leave me?"

The rocking began to ease and she looked around, panic-stricken. Where was she? It was pitch black – far too dark to see. She cried out for help, but the noise of the storm drowned out her words.

Di must have dozed off again, because when she lifted her head the next time, the sun was beginning to rise and Di found she wasn't lying on a board at all. In fact, she wasn't even lying down; she was standing with her cheek pressed up against…a door! It was small – not much larger than Di, and shaped like an arch. It was ornately carved with the picture of a woman's head. Then Di's heart stopped for what seemed like ten full seconds. She'd noticed, below the head, a single word carved into the wood:

"*Diana*"

Di gulped. She stared at the door for some time. Her name. The voices had called it. It was written on the door.

"Why me?" she wailed. "Why does it want me?"

The Haunted Door

With a thumping heart, Di pushed the door as
hard as she could. It didn't budge. She turned to look
behind her and gasped in horror. This definitely wasn't
the Highwayman Inn. She was in some kind of cabin.
Its walls were sloping and there were ship's instruments
everywhere. The benches and tables were fixed to the
floor. And, although the oil lamps on the tables were
unlit, the rising sun shone through them, casting an
eerie pink glow. She remembered the rocking from
earlier. She was on board a ship! But how had she got
there? And how was she going to find her way back to
the Inn – and her family?

A small door at the opposite end of the cabin slowly
began to creak open. Di held her breath, steeling
herself for the awful truth. Some horrible creature was
holding her captive, perhaps

an evil pirate captain, zombies, or… vampires!

Fingers curled round
the edge of door. They

47

looked quite ordinary. In fact, the ring on the second finger seemed familiar. A pale, anxious face peered around the door.

"Mum!" Di shrieked. She flew into her mother's arms. "Where am I? What happened? ...and pleeeease can we go home now?"

Mum wrinkled her forehead in confusion.

"You're in the pub, love. I suppose you were sleepwalking again," Mum told her. "This is the breakfast room. It's only used for overnight guests, and as we're the only ones staying here, we just hadn't opened it up. The old owner decorated it to look like a ship's cabin. It's very realistic, isn't it?"

Di didn't answer.

"I'm not just sleepwalking, Mum," she explained. "Something is pulling me around the house. I think it wants something from me, but I don't know what.

Pleeease can we go home?" she begged

again. Mum nodded slowly. "I promise," she sighed. "Just one more night, then we'll definitely go home."

That night Di ached with tiredness, but she couldn't sleep, afraid of what might happen.

"Hold my hand," Em suggested. "Then if anything, or anyone, tries to take you away, I'll pull you back." Di smiled at her little sister, and the two girls fell asleep side by side, snuggled next to one another, their arms and fingers twisted together.

Before she knew it, Di was awake. It had happened again; she was back at the door with her face pressed against it. Once more the cabin was rocking. And once more the voice was calling her name. It sounded clearer this time. A boy's voice maybe? Not the old man she had imagined, with the rough, fisherman's hands.

It was only when the rocking died down, and the sun began to rise, that Di realised she was still holding Em's hand. Em hadn't saved Di from the dream, she had come with her!

Di tightened her grip on her little sister's hands, but the light was still dim, she couldn't see her. And somehow Em seemed to be on the other side of the door. But then the burning began again, just on her left hand. She felt small fingers, but they were rough and weathered. They were pressing on her arm. They were trying to pull her through door.

"No!" she cried, "leave me alone!" But the hand

kept pulling and pulling. She could see it now… and it was hideous! The fingers were black, the nails and fingertips were missing. The backs of the hands were almost purple, with dark, black scabs. They kept on pulling, and Di kicked and wriggled and scratched, but she couldn't get free.

Di heard a cry from behind her, and a figure hurled itself at the door. It growled and bit into the blackened hand, and all at once the hand melted away. Di shivered and sobbed with relief, her left hand was red, bruised and sore, but Em was still clinging on to her other hand. Her brave little sister had bitten the ghost! And sent him packing…for now.

As the family's car rolled off along the road to Okehampton later that day, Di's relief to be leaving was mixed with a kind of regret. She'd never know why the ghost had picked on her, why he'd called her name, or what on earth that door had to do with it all.

But the answer wasn't so far away, if only Di had known where to look. Upstairs in the inn, on a dusty old shelf, one book had lain open for years. The pages were faded and crumbling, but they told a fascinating tale…

Some 170 years before, an old whaling ship had been dashed to pieces on an iceberg. The entire crew went down with the boat but only one body was ever found. He was young – a cabin boy perhaps? Washed ashore, the boy clung, with blackened, frost-bitten fingers, to the single piece of wreckage that remained of the ship. It was a small, carved wooden door, with the face of a woman at the top, and the name of the ship carved below it. Just one word…Diana.

Something Fishy...

The house at 46 Cowick Street, Exeter, was a newsagent's for over 90 years though it has been standing for more like 200 years. There are several stories of hauntings here, including strange goings-on in the understairs cupboard...

"I don't want to go!" Nan was being stubborn. At nearly 90 years old, she still wasn't ready to move to an old people's home. She wanted to stay in her own home, the old newsagent's shop at the top of Cowick Street that looked well past its sell-by date.

Polly and her mum and dad had been summoned for a family meeting at Nan's house. They had arrived by train, meeting up with her Aunty Jenny and her cousins, Maisie and Sophie, on the way.

Her other cousins, Alice and Ben Salter, lived just round the corner from Nan's, in Powderham Road. For most of Polly's eleven years, the two sides of the family hadn't spoken. She had no idea why. Alice and Ben eyed her from the opposite corner of the room. She'd never met them before, but she knew her other cousins well. She'd always got on with eight-year-old Maisie, but Sophie was two months younger than

Polly and they'd never liked each other very much.

The grown-ups were arguing within half an hour and when Nan suggested the children go off and play, Polly felt glad to escape. As Polly and her cousins trooped up the stairs, Nan called after them.

"You can go anywhere but the basement, mind," she said. Polly wouldn't dare go where she shouldn't. She found the old house creepy at the best of times.

The wallpaper on the stairs was peeling in the corners. It was a funny browny-yellow colour that had maybe once been cream, with small brown flowers that had maybe once been red. The carpet on the creaky stairs was frayed and in places you could see the dusty floorboards underneath. The old house hadn't been loved since Great-Grandad had died, almost 30 years ago!

"What shall we play?" Maisie asked.

"Well, it's the perfect house for hide-and-seek," said Polly.

Sophie had wasted no time making friends with Alice. They kept whispering and giggling together, though Sophie was quite definitely 'in charge'. Ben was the youngest. He seemed sweet, but outnumbered, being the only boy.

"Hide-and-seek is so dull," Sophie whinged.

"Let's give it a go," said Maisie. "I'll be the seeker."

The cousins scattered about the first floor of the house, hiding behind curtains, in dusty alcoves and under rickety tables. Alice and Sophie hid together, but Maisie found them almost straight away, which made Sophie sulk.

"I vote we play Sardines this time," Sophie announced, after everyone had finally been found.

"Sardines?" said Ben. "Never heard of it."

"It's like hide-and-seek, but four of us count and only one person hides. Once you find the person, you hide with them."

"The last person to find them is the loser," Alice explained.

"Cool," Ben whistled. "Let's play."

Maisie and Polly looked at each other and shrugged.

Something Fishy...

"OK," said Sophie, delighted to be in charge. "Alice can hide, while the rest of us count." Polly saw Sophie wink at Alice and knew something fishy was going on.

"Ninety-nine, a hundred." Ben shrieked, lifting his hands from his eyes.

"Right," said Sophie, "Ben and Maisie can search this floor. Polly, you do the top floor, and I'll try downstairs."

"I'd rather go with Polly," Maisie complained, but Sophie always had an answer.

"You can't leave poor little Ben on his own," she said, flouncing off before anyone could argue.

"Don't worry," Polly told Maisie. "I'll be OK."

But she climbed the stairs with her heart thumping fiercely. Each room on the top floor was stacked high with old papers. A dust cloud drifted into the air as Polly tripped over a pile accidentally. She knew she'd been set up; Alice wasn't here. But she wanted to prove to Sophie that she wasn't scared. Anyway, she wasn't scared – she was absolutely terrified. On her own, the house seemed spookier than ever.

A sudden breeze lifted Polly's hair and she let out a gasp. A tiny window was open to the elements, inviting in the cold autumn air. She sighed with relief when she saw it, closed it with trembling hands and then hurried back down the stairs.

No one was on the first floor. Polly poked about in a few of the rooms and moved down to the ground floor. There were raised voices in the sitting room still, and the door to the shop was firmly locked. Where else could anyone hide? Her heart stopped for a moment when she realised where her cousins had gone.

The basement, Polly said to herself. *Sophie knew I wouldn't like it, so she got Alice to hide down there.* She placed her hand on the top of the handrail. That stopped it shaking at least. Everything was quiet suddenly. Even the grown-ups sounded muffled and distant. She could clearly hear her own heart thumping, though.

She began to move forward, but it was as though something was stopping her. I'm the oldest, she reminded herself. The others went down without making a fuss, so I can too.

Polly's hand gripped harder on the rail. The heating was on full blast, so why were her arms prickling with goose pimples? Breathing in, Polly caught a waft of unfamiliar scent. It was sweet, flowery, not unpleasant at all, but somehow she knew it was coming from another place...another time. It made her flesh creep and her blood run cold. Her hand wouldn't lift from the handrail.

"Pull yourself together, Pol." She said it out loud, as if to prove she wasn't afraid. And with what seemed superhuman effort, she wrenched her hand away from the handrail at last and lifted her foot to move down the stairs. Every movement seemed to happen in slow motion. The thin air in front of her was a wall she had to push through, whilst her feet seemed glued to the stairs. It took an eternity to reach the bottom and all the time her heart thumped wildly.

Something Fishy...

The basement was a mess. Long strings of cobwebs hung from the ceiling and gathered on the peeling plaster in the corners. There must have been at least ten good hiding places down here, but somehow Polly knew where everyone was hiding.

The door didn't fit properly. It looked homemade. The padlock had rusted away. Now, instead of pushing against the air, Polly felt pulled, drawn in – by an understairs cupboard! She heard nothing, but, strangely, she knew the children had hidden inside.

Panic seized Polly. *Why can't I hear them?* she thought. They must be in danger – I've got to get them out of there! She clutched at the padlock, scratching the door with her well-chewed fingernails as she did so and…it happened right in front of her eyes. The new door seemed to melt away and morph into rough, old splintery boards, so carelessly hammered across the cupboard doorway that some of the nails were bent and loose. No matter how hard Polly pulled, though, the boards wouldn't come away. And in any case, the children were nowhere to be seen.

Instead, something – she couldn't say what – was seeping through the boards, slowly wrapping around her, like an icy blanket. It held her so tightly she could hardly move or breathe. She felt fingers of ice squeezing her heart and her throat. She struggled to escape, gasping for breath, but found herself staring, wide-eyed, through the gaps in the boards.

Two dark eyes stared back. She looked closer. The eyes were desperate and pleading. They bored into her. There was a boy inside the cupboard – and it wasn't Ben. He was dark-skinned, he wore strange-looking clothes and he was drawing her in...

Polly was paralysed, hypnotised. She stared at the boy for what may have been seconds but felt like for ever. At last, something furry and warm brushed against her leg, releasing her from the icy blanket. And she could breathe again. Dropping her hand, she touched something soft. It licked her leg. A dog! Polly almost grinned with relief, but when she looked down, there was nothing to see... The dog had melted away leaving just the faintest whiff of perfume...it soothed her and brought her to her senses...

Where were her cousins? Had the cupboard somehow taken them away somewhere?

Polly's stomach knotted. She scratched frantically at the boards again, and it was as though a spell was suddenly broken. The air warmed and the boards suddenly became a clumsy door – that burst open:

"Loser..."
"Ha, ha, got you!"
"We won!"

"Poor Polly, you were looking for hours!"

All four children came tumbling out of the cupboard. Laughing, smiling, pointing, giggling, they hurried back upstairs, leaving Polly staring into the space they left behind them. It was just a cupboard, an ordinary understairs cupboard. It was clean – no cobwebs at all – and empty. But she knew she hadn't imagined those feelings; she could still see the boy in her mind.

Something made Polly look up. The children had gone back upstairs, but their shouts and laughter seemed to linger after them. Why hadn't they felt anything?

Nan was smiling down from the top of the stairs. She was leaning heavily on the handrail, but holding out a hand for her great-granddaughter to grasp.

Something Fishy...

"There are some things you ought to know," she said. "But first, tell me everything you saw."

Nan sat on a stool in the shop, while Polly told her story. The old lady didn't seem at all surprised.

"It's one of the reasons I don't want to leave," Nan began. "Some say Cowick Street is as old as the Romans! It was an important route into Exeter from the west. This building is only a couple of hundred years old, though. It used to be a coaching inn – a place for travellers to rest for the night. So these walls have witnessed many things. Some good, some bad. Like you, I was afraid at first, but I've got used to the ghosts now. They're mostly friendly."

"But who are they?" asked Polly.

"Well, there's old Mrs Perriam, who used to own the shop. She died – ooh – 50, maybe 60 years ago. She brings her little dog."

"Why did she come back today?" Polly couldn't understand it.

"I think she was looking after you. She and I discovered the cupboard together," chuckled Nan. "We both had the gift. Though we never knew why that place chilled our bones so badly."

"And the boy," Polly asked, desperately. "Who was he?"

"He might have been a slave," said Nan. "He was

obviously treated badly, but some questions can never be answered."

Polly was having difficulty taking everything in. At last she sighed, relieved that it was over.

"Oh, Nan, wouldn't it be best if you moved?" she said, clutching her great-grandmother's hand. "I never want to experience anything like that again."

Nan placed her other hand soothingly on top of Polly's. "You may think that now, Polly," she said gently. "But you're like me. You've got the gift."

Polly looked at the old lady blankly. "What gift?"

"A sixth sense

– the ability to see spirits that other people don't," Nan explained, jerking her head towards the room full of relatives. "Your side of the family has it, the other side doesn't. That's why the Salters think I should leave here. I know you'll understand – one day."

Polly felt a new kind of horror creeping across her flesh.

"I'm not sure I follow you, Nan," she said. Nan took a deep breath.

"Well, my lovely. Today was your first experience of spirit life but mark my words…" she gave Polly's hand a squeeze. "It certainly won't be your last."

The Spanish Girl

A plaque above the door of Torre Abbey's Spanish Barn tells of the terrible tragedy that happened there around 400 years ago. Some people have even seen the ghost that still haunts the area, in search of a lost love...

"Everybody off!" The coach slowed to a stop on The King's Drive and 30 pupils from St Margaret's Primary School trooped in through the gate and onto the tarmac to the side of Torre Abbey. Today should have been a treat for them all, but Gemma Palk was in a foul mood.

Mrs Hannaford was down from Totnes for the day. She usually taught at Dartington College of Arts, but she was setting up a new art project which would help the Year Six children 'express themselves through art'. Her favourite expression was, "Don't draw what you see, draw what you feel!" And it was what Gemma disliked most about her.

Art was what Gemma did best. Her family and all her friends said so. And, until now, all her teachers had said so too. Gemma was great at drawing things – as long as they didn't move. Still life they called it: a bowl of fruit, an old shoe. She could copy photographs no problem; trees, flowers and scenery too.

But Mrs Hannaford turned her nose up at Gemma's perfect drawings.

"You might as well just take a photograph," she'd sniff. "Where's your passion, Gemma? What do you feel?"

Leave me alone, I'm only ten, Gemma wanted to say. But she wasn't quite brave enough.

The rest of the Year Sixes loved Mrs Hannaford's lessons, she was always telling them stories – or off in fantasy land, as Gemma called it.

"Let's see what we can find," she was enthusing now. "Part of Torre Abbey has been restored magnificently. There's the ruined church and gardens to explore and the section of the house where the Cary family lived. Choose something that shows us a bit of history. Pick your own subject – a room, a window, a piece of furniture – and draw it in your own style. Try to really feel it."

Suddenly, the rest of the class all seemed to be brilliant at art. Whatever they did, Mrs Hannaford thought it was fantastic. Gemma was the one who was struggling. She watched them all chattering excitedly as they marched through the crumbling arch of the old gatehouse. She hung back as they disappeared into the main entrance of the abbey and then turned and walked off in the opposite direction.

The old barn didn't look like anything special. It was a tall brick building with just a few very long thin windows. Its huge doors were padlocked shut. She wandered around it aimlessly and discovered that one

of the smaller side doors was slightly open. She didn't know why she did it, but she squeezed through the narrow gap and sneaked inside.

There wasn't much to see: red brick walls, with patterned floor tiles and a high wooden roof that looked like the up-turned hull of a ship. The building was more or less an empty shell, though it looked like someone was setting up an exhibition in there, because large display screens blocked the view to the far end of the barn.

A sign somewhere said that the barn was built in 1196, but Gemma didn't take much notice of that. She was too busy feeling sorry for herself. *I'm not going to bother with drawing any more*, she thought to herself, as she stood in front of a busy display screen. There was a hubbub in the background: chattering, mumblings in some foreign language, a few people seemed to be arguing – it sounded like a coach-load of Spanish tourists. There were certainly plenty of them, and Gemma wanted to keep well out of their way.

She was staring at the display for some time before she noticed the girl standing next to her, smiling kindly even though she looked heart-broken. Her eyes were red-rimmed. Had she been crying?

"You look so patiently at this picture," the girl said, and she sniffed a little. "I see you are very interested in the Spanish Armada." She had a funny way of saying Armada. She said 'thees' instead of this and 'peeshur' instead of picture. She must have been one of the Spanish tourists.

To be honest, Gemma hadn't even been looking at the picture. She'd been off in her own angry world. Now she examined it more closely, she saw a whole fleet of old-fashioned ships, their sails billowing in the wind. She'd heard of the Spanish Armada, but she didn't have a clue what it was.

The girl seemed to read Gemma's mind because, almost immediately, she started telling her all about it.

"The Armada set sail over 400 years ago," she began. "Our Catholic King, Philip of Spain, wanted to overthrow your Protestant English Queen, your Elizabeth I, yes?" Gemma couldn't help tutting. Of course she knew about Elizabeth I. She even knew that Catholics and Protestants had different views about the Christian religion.

"Philip sent a great fleet of ships to invade your country. The sailors on board, they were more scared of pirate attacks than of your English navy – they were so sure they would win!" She had a faraway look in her eye. "Some even took their wives and girlfriends with them, ready to set up home when they conquered England." She pointed out a ship in the picture. "Nuestra Senora del Rosario," she said, in fast, fluent Spanish. In the picture, the Spanish fleet sailed in a semi-circle, but this ship was lagging behind. "It had a crash," the girl explained, "and fell out of line from the rest of the ships. Your Francis Drake captured it and towed it into Torbay harbour. The

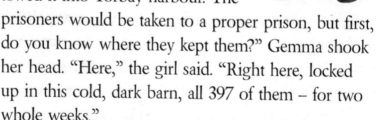

prisoners would be taken to a proper prison, but first, do you know where they kept them?" Gemma shook her head. "Here," the girl said. "Right here, locked up in this cold, dark barn, all 397 of them – for two whole weeks."

Gemma glanced around the barn. She couldn't imagine staying here for one night, let alone fourteen.

"And were there women prisoners too?" she asked.

"Only one," the girl gave a sad smile and repeated, "only one."

"Gemma, we've been looking for you everywhere!" Olivia came bursting into the barn through a small door on the opposite side.

"You'd better come, quick, Mrs Hannaford's going ballistic!"

Gemma felt a sudden pang of guilt for wandering off. She didn't feel angry any more, the Spanish girl had really distracted her. Right at that moment, though, Gemma forgot all about her, as she rushed after Olivia, past the screens, and through the other door. She was a bit surprised that there was no sign of the Spanish coach party – they'd been chattering away in the background the whole time she was in the barn – but she didn't think any more about it as she hurried back to her classmates.

Mrs Hannaford was so relieved to see Gemma that she didn't get cross. Gemma was quiet on the bus on the way home, though. She wasn't angry. She was thinking. Thinking about how much she wanted to draw. Not now, though. She needed to get home first, and work in her bedroom, away from everyone else.

That evening, Gemma picked up a piece of charcoal and opened her sketchbook, stared at it for a few moments, and then she began. Her hand flew across the page – it sounds stupid, but it was as if the charcoal was in control. She wasn't sure what she was drawing – it felt like someone, or something, was guiding her hand. At first, it looked like she'd just scribbled a load of lines on the page, but then, gradually, the picture started to take shape. There were two dark, watery eyes, a long, elegant nose and curls of thick, wavy black hair. She was drawing the girl; the Spanish girl she'd met in the barn.

"Wow!" Olivia said the next day, looking at the picture as they lined up for class. "That's amazing, Gemma, it's your best drawing ever. But how did you get her to look like...a ghost? Who is she?"

"It's the girl I was talking to in the barn yesterday," Gemma said.

"What girl?" said Olivia. Gemma looked at the picture again. Hadn't Olivia seen the girl when she came in? The hairs prickled on the back of her neck. Why did Olivia think she looked like a ghost?

Gemma wasn't expecting Mrs Hannaford to be in class and by the time she spotted her, striding across the playground towards them, it was too late to hide the picture. Gemma waited for her criticism. But it didn't come. Instead she studied it for a moment, and then she said, with real delight, "You've done it, Gemma, you've really done it! I always knew you could."

"What d'you mean?" Gemma tried to hide her smile. She hadn't realised it, but all she'd wanted from the start was Mrs Hannaford's approval.

The Spanish Girl

"You've used your talent for detail, but you've let your emotions show through. Look at the sadness in her eyes, and her skin, it looks translucent – how did you do that? You must have put a good deal of research into finding out about the legend..."

"Legend, what legend?" asked Gemma. Mrs Hannaford was obviously off in fantasy land again.

"She's the Spanish girl who was captured with the crew of Nuestra Senora del Rosario, isn't she?" she said. "That's why you've drawn her in men's clothes, isn't it?"

"Oooh, I heard that story too," Olivia chipped in. "They brought her to the Spanish Barn because they thought she was one of the men. She wanted to stay with her boyfriend."

Gemma hadn't really looked at the Spanish girl properly yesterday. Now she thought about it, she realised the girl had been wearing odd clothes.

"Of course, it all came to a tragic end," said Mrs Hannaford, sighed. "The prisoners got sick and the girl was the first to die. She was so young, and so beautiful – exactly as your picture shows – and they reckon she never left the barn."

Olivia took up the story. "Oh yes," she enthused. "She still wanders the Spanish Barn, sobbing her poor heart out..."

"Really?" Gemma was starting to feel a bit wobbly as they started moving into the classroom.

"Are you feeling all right?" asked Olivia. Gemma was relieved to make it to her desk. She was sitting down now, but her legs wouldn't stop shaking.

There was no Spanish coach party. Gemma thought to herself. Those voices I heard, they were the prisoners from 400 years ago! And I had a conversation with a ghost... The freakiest thing is that I'm glad I did, because she showed me that I really can draw!

The Ragged Boy

Lyn and Exmoor Museum can be found in a charming whitewashed cottage that is probably the oldest in Lynton. But once upon a time, this cottage was a children's home. One of the children went missing and a 'nasty lady' was said to haunt one of the old bedrooms...

Dan knew immediately that the boy was a ghost. He almost laughed, it was so obvious. The boy was standing right in the middle of Market Street, in front of the old cottage museum, and looking right at him. He was ragged, just like a character from Oliver Twist. His clothes were all the wrong sizes: tight jacket, ragged shirt, frayed trousers. They were really grubby too. He only had one boot, on his left foot – oh, and you could see straight through him!

Dan was coming back from his guitar lesson, after school on a Tuesday. It was halfway through the Autumn term, and the clocks had just gone back. He'd never walked home on his own in the dark. He hadn't even got very far, because Lynton Primary School was opposite the pretty little whitewashed cottage that housed the Lyn and Exmoor Museum. Apparently, the cottage was Lynton's oldest surviving home. So maybe Dan shouldn't have been surprised to find a ghost standing outside. But he felt far more surprised than afraid.

The sight of the ghost made Dan tingle all over, but it was the kind of fun-scared feeling you get from reading a really good horror story. He couldn't wait to tell his mates about it.

The boy was there again the following Tuesday, at exactly the same time, just as Dan was walking home from his guitar lesson. And this time he seemed to be trying to communicate. His lips didn't move or anything, but he kind of made thoughts happen in Dan's mind. "Help me, you've got to help me!" the boy seemed to be saying. Then he looked back, nervously, towards the cottage and even though the museum had closed a good half hour earlier, he ran back inside, straight through the locked front door!

Weeks went by and the boy didn't appear again. But Dan always thought about him on his way home each Tuesday, with the strap of his guitar slung across his chest. He'd been really getting into the lessons. He'd even persuaded his teacher to help him form a band with his friends: Toby on keyboards and Ethan on drums. They had their first rehearsal one Tuesday in November. Mrs Bale had been impressed and told them they showed a lot of promise. She even said: "Come up with a good name for yourselves, and you

can play at the school Christmas concert."

So that's what they were talking about as they wandered towards the school gates.

"How about something to do with school," said Ethan. "Seeing as that's where we'll be performing."

"The Lyntons," Toby tried. "Hmm, it's a possibility." But he didn't sound convinced.

"Or what about the things that make the town famous. The flood, or the cliff railway," Dan suggested.

"Yeah, but they don't sound exciting, and anyway,

not everyone wants to remember the flood!"

"There's always the Valley of Rocks," Ethan said. The valley was about a mile and a half out of the village, and there were some seriously weird rock formations there.

"That's a better idea," said Toby. "Some of the rocks have great names – the Devil's Cheese Ring and Ragged Jack."

"The Devil's Cheese Ring!" Dan laughed out loud. "That's an awesome name for a band."

"You think so?" Ethan raised an eyebrow.

They were laughing and joking and chattering excitedly, so they didn't see the boy to begin with. He was hopping from his bare right foot onto his leather-booted left foot, as if he needed the loo.

Ethan, who was walking a little ahead of the others, spotted him first.

"Woah!" he stopped dead pushing his arms back, straight, as a sign for the others not to come any closer.

The boy was pointing back towards the house.

"W-who is he?" Toby asked.

"That's him," Dan said, as he looked up. "The ghost boy I told you about." He was delighted his mates could see the ghost too.

"She's coming," the boy was saying in Dan's head.

The others heard it too. He was pointing back at the house, looking anxious.

Dan smiled. "He's not at all scary, is he?" Ethan and Toby didn't seem so sure.

"You've got to help me," the boy said in their heads. "She's going to get me!" He pointed towards the house again. And then they saw it! Everything happened so fast. The front door of the house literally blasted open and out flew this...thing. It didn't look like anything to begin with. It was just a fast-moving mist, or a wind, or something... But then it dropped down next to the ragged boy and, as it stopped, it shifted, taking the shape of a hideous old woman.

Her wide-brimmed bonnet and long green dress were at least a hundred years out of date, but they were the most normal things about her. Her face was half scabby flesh, half skeleton. One eye looked piercing, and evil – the boys felt it boring into them – the other wasn't an eye at all, it was just a socket, bloody and empty.

The old woman's left hand was covered with a black, leather glove. Her right hand had no glove – and no flesh either. It was all skeleton. But a skeleton that was somehow alive, and working all too well, because tight in its grip was a large, cast-iron frying pan. The pan was heavy, but the woman had no

trouble lifting it. And the pan was sizzling hot too, but those finger-bones didn't feel the heat.

Suddenly, the old woman began to dissolve. She was moving again – towards the boys this time! She whirled in a misty blur towards them, and above the mist they could still see the frying pan – hot and heavy and coming straight for them.

The boys had never run so fast in their lives. Dan felt his throat tighten. He was choking! He'd been caught! But it was just his guitar strap tightening round his neck. Toby tripped over his own feet and nearly sprawled on the floor. Ethan felt his legs buckling underneath him. The three boys ran like toddlers, screaming for their mums: one home to Lydgate Lane, one to Cross Street, the other to Burvill Street.

Dan crashed in through his front door, his face ashen, his whole body shaking. He slammed it shut, and then peered back anxiously through the letterbox to see if the 'thing' was following him. It wasn't. He sank to his knees with relief. Then he panicked – what about Ethan and Toby! It might have caught one of them!

Later, Dan told his mum everything. He wouldn't normally – he never liked to worry her, but he was so scared he didn't think. As Dan heard himself talking, he thought how ridiculous it all sounded. Why should anyone believe him? But his mum just stood quietly and listened. When he stopped talking, she put a calming hand on his shoulder.

"I'm going to phone the police," she said.

Dan thought that was a stupid idea. They'd never believe his story in a million years! Even if they did, what could they do?

But to Dan's amazement, the police came straight away. Other people had seen things too. The old woman was terrorising the village and, somehow, she had to be stopped.

Dan wasn't quite sure how it happened, but he found himself agreeing to go to the cottage with the police. The ragged boy had asked for help, and Dan didn't like letting people down.

Now, as he stood on the very spot where the 'thing' had chased him, Dan really wished he'd stayed at home like Ethan and Toby. What if the 'thing' came after him again? What if it got him this time? He'd once heard the phrase, 'quaking in my boots'. "That's what I'm doing now," he thought, his legs shaking.

The police brought a 'medium' with them – a lady who said she could 'talk' to the dead. Dan had never met anyone like her in his life, and he couldn't take his

eyes off her. She didn't really look at things, she sort of
felt them. Not with her fingers and hands, but with her
'emotions'. She worked her way around the cottage,
closing her eyes, taking deep breaths and standing for
a few moments in each room. Then she'd shake her
head and move on.

At last, she stopped and pressed her foot on a
floorboard. It creaked and moved slightly under
her weight. Everyone gathered round. Dan's heart
hammered in his chest. What on earth had she found?

The medium went quiet at first. Then she went
weird. Her eyes rolled round in their sockets, her body

hung, limply, like a rag doll, and she began to wail and moan. The sound grew louder and louder, and Dan stood next to her, paralysed with shock and fear.

At last, she threw back her head and her body straightened. A green light was seeping up through gap in the floorboards. It crept up the medium's body, enveloping her in its eerie glow. Dan watched in horror. He could hardly believe what he saw because, as the light advanced, she was, very gradually, turning into the hideous old woman in the green dress and bonnet.

It was then that he fainted.

Dan took the rest of the week off school. Not because he was ill; more because he was embarrassed – word would have got round, everyone would know about the fainting. But he was upset too, because they'd found stuff under the floorboards: a tatty leather boot, a large cast-iron frying pan, and a pile of small, human bones. The discovery seemed to have chased the old woman's spirit away.

Dan tried not to think about what had happened to the ghost boy. Instead he tried to think of a way people might remember him. By the time Ethan and Toby came round, at the end of the week, Dan had cheered up a lot.

"Are we still going to do the concert then, guys?" he asked. "'Cos I've got a great name for the band."

In the next couple of weeks, the boys practised like crazy and by the day of the concert, they were really pleased with their act. They stood backstage that night, a jangle of nerves and excitement, as Mrs Bale walked out and spoke to the audience.

"Ladies and gentlemen, boys and girls," she said. "It's their very first gig, and I know you're going to love them, so please give a very warm welcome to Lynton Primary's very own...

Ragged Boys!"

Spooky Devon

Ghastly Jokes

If you're feeling frightful after reading about spooky Devon, here are some jokes to make you jolly!

What do you call the ghost of a door-to-door salesman?
A dead ringer.

What did the mother ghost say to the baby ghost?
'Don't spook until you're spooken to.'

What do little ghosts drink?
Evaporated milk.

When do ghosts usually appear?
Just before someone screams.

What do ghosts serve for dessert?
Ice Scream.

What kind of mistakes do ghosts make?
Boo boos.

What's a ghoul's favourite game?
Hide-and-shriek!

Ghastly Jokes

What's a ghost's favourite ride at the carnival?
The roller-ghoster.

Where do ghosts post their letters?
At the Ghost Office.

What kind of street does a ghost like best?
A dead end!

Why did the ghost cross the road?
To get to 'The Other Side'.

What do you call a ghost's mother and father?
Transparents!

Why are ghosts bad at telling lies?
Because you can see right through them!

What did the ghost teacher say to her class?
Look at the board and I'll go through it again.

What is a ghost's favourite day of the week?
Frightday!

When does a ghost have breakfast?
In the moaning.

Ghost Locator

Where? Exeter Cathedral
When? 1864
What was it like then? Not much different from today. The present cathedral was built about 1360 and the minstrel's gallery dates from that time.
Find it in: The Minstrel's Gallery

Where? B3212 in the Dartmoor National Park
When? Since 1910
What was it like then? An old turnpike road between Postbridge and Princetown that cut across the moor through Two Bridges.
Find it in: Hairy Hands

Where? The 13th century Highwayman Inn, Sourton, Okehampton
When? 170 years ago.
What was it like then? The haunted door came from a wooden whaling ship, *Diana*, that was wrecked off the Lincolnshire coast.
Find it in: The Haunted Door

Where? Perriam's Newsagents, 46 Cowick Street, Exeter
When? The Pack Horse Inn until 1897; Perriam's until 2006.
What was it like then? An old building with a shop on the ground floor, living space above...and a cellar below!
Find it in: Something Fishy...

Where? The Spanish Barn, Torre Abbey, Torquay
When? 1588
What was it like then? A vast, stone barn with huge wooden beams supporting the roof, already 200 years old when the Spanish captives arrived.
Find it in: The Spanish Girl

Where? St Vincent's Cottage, Market Street, Lynton
When? 1847
What was it like then? A stone cottage in a sleepy fishing village.
Find it in: The Ragged Boy

Sleep tight!

Acknowledgements

Cover and page 10: Andreas Meyer/Shutterstock; page 26: Martin Fowler/Shutterstock; pages 28-29: David Young/Shutterstock; page 51: jeka84/Shutterstock; page 53: Mansurova Yulia/Shutterstock; page 54: Tim Sutcliffe; page 68: Alegria/Shutterstock; pages 70-71: Alegria/Booka/jara3000/Shutterstock; page 74: Leo Brown; page 80: David Luscombe/Shutterstock; pages 82/83: Nowik/Shutterstock and Pavel K/Shutterstock pages 90/91: pdesign/Shutterstock

Disclaimer